Olympia
the Games
Fairy

Join the **Rainbow Magic Reading Challenge!**

Read the story and collect your fairy points to climb the
Reading Rainbow at the back of the book.

This book is worth 2 stars.

Special thanks to
Narinder Dhami

ORCHARD BOOKS

First published in Great Britain in 2012 by The Watts Publishing Group
This edition published in 2021 by The Watts Publishing Group

9 10 8

© 2012 Rainbow Magic Limited.
© 2012 HIT Entertainment Limited.
Illustrations © 2012 The Watts Publishing Group Limited.

A CIP catalogue record for this book is available from the British Library.

ISBN 978 1 40831 596 5

Printed and bound in Great Britain by Clays Ltd, Elcograf S.p.A

MIX
Paper from
responsible sources
FSC
www.fsc.org   FSC® C104740

The paper and board used in this book are made from wood from responsible sources.

Orchard Books
An imprint of Hachette Children's Group
Part of The Watts Publishing Group Limited
Carmelite House, 50 Victoria Embankment, London EC4Y 0DZ

An Hachette UK Company
www.hachette.co.uk
www.hachettechildrens.co.uk

Olympia
the Games
Fairy

By Daisy Meadows

ORCHARD

www.orchardseriesbooks.co.uk

Jack Frost's
Ice Castle

Cycle route

Running route

Winners' podium

Contents

Story Two:
The Musical Bicycle Bell

Story Three:
The Tireless Trainers

Jack Frost's Spell

I want to cycle and swim and run,
And I have to win or it's simply no fun.
But I don't want to train and have aching feet,
I'd much rather steal and lie and cheat!

Olympia's magic can give me a hand,
So, goblins, off to Fairyland!
We'll steal her magical objects away,
Then lots of medals will come my way!

The sparkling swimming cap makes you swim fast,
In the tireless trainers I'll never come last.
I'll win with the musical bicycle bell,
I'm going for gold, as you can tell!

Story One
The Sparkling
Swimming Cap

Chapter One
Swimming Surprise

"This is going to be really exciting!" Kirsty Tate said, beaming at her best friend, Rachel Walker. Kirsty had just arrived in Tippington to stay with Rachel for part of the summer holidays. "It's the first time I've ever been to a – a—" Kirsty stopped, looking confused.

"*What* did you say this sporting event was called, Rachel?"

Her friend laughed. "A triathlon," she reminded Kirsty as Mr Walker turned the car down a street signposted *To the river*. "All the athletes take part in swimming, cycling and running races, one after the other. They don't even get a break in between! That's right, isn't it, Mum?"

"Yes," replied Mrs Walker from the passenger seat. "They go from one event straight into the next."

Kirsty's eyes opened wide. "Wow, they must be super-fit!" she exclaimed.

"I think we're going to be exhausted just cheering them on," joked Mr Walker, who was now searching for an empty space in the packed car park.

The triathlon was taking place in the pretty riverside town of Melford, not far from Tippington. As they all climbed out of the car, Kirsty admired the little thatched cottages and the stone-built church with its square belltower. It was

a perfect summer's day with a brilliant-blue sky and sunshine streaming down.

"There are loads of people here," Rachel remarked, as they followed the crowds down the street. Ahead of them the girls could see a long waterfront with

 an ancient stone bridge spanning the wide river. A set of steps led down to the edge of the river, and there were men and women in swimming costumes and colourful swimming caps standing on

the steps, waiting eagerly for the race to start.

A large audience had already gathered. There were spectators sitting on banks of wooden seats, and some were also standing on the bridge.

"How far do they have to swim?" asked Kirsty.

"See that yellow buoy bobbing around further down the river?" Mrs Walker pointed it out to the girls. "The athletes circle around that and come back to where they are now. It's about 750 metres."

"And then they dry themselves off and

jump on their
bikes for the
next part
of the
triathlon,"
Rachel's
dad added.

Nearby was
a roped-off area that enclosed racks of
bicycles with helmets hanging on the
handlebars. "The cycle race is twenty
kilometres long."

"Oh, I'm getting tired just thinking
about it all!" Kirsty sighed, making
Rachel laugh.

"Ladies and gentlemen," boomed
a voice from a loudspeaker attached
to one of the lampposts, "the Melford
Triathlon will begin in five minutes! Will

all the competitors take up their starting positions, please?"

Rachel and Kirsty watched as the swimmers jostled a little for position at the bottom of the steps. The girls also noticed several small boats bobbing around close by, manned by people in white baseball caps with *Melford Triathlon* written on the peaks in blue.

Rachel guessed that they were the

stewards, and that it was their job to make sure the events ran smoothly.

"Mum, could Kirsty and I watch from the riverside?" asked Rachel eagerly. "Then we can get a *really* good view of the race."

Her mum nodded. "We'll see you back here later," she told them. "Then we'll go and have a cream tea at one of the cafes in Melford."

While Mr and Mrs Walker found some spare seats, Kirsty and Rachel hurried

along the
waterfront
to an
empty
spot near
a large
clump of
reeds.

"Isn't this
magical?" Kirsty
remarked. Sunbeams glinted on the
rippling water and the girls could see
shimmering blue and green dragonflies
dancing across its surface.

"Talking of magic, I wonder if we'll
see our fairy friends this summer?"
Rachel said hopefully.

"Oh, wouldn't that be great!" Kirsty
exclaimed, her eyes lighting up. She and

Rachel loved being secret friends with the fairies, and together they'd had some marvellous, magical adventures.

At that moment there was the sound of a piercing whistle, followed by loud splashes as all the swimmers plunged into the river.

There were cheers and whoops from the crowd, and Rachel and Kirsty joined in.

But as the swimmers set off towards the yellow marker, something very strange happened. Half of the athletes spun around in the water and began heading in the *opposite* direction. Meanwhile almost all the remaining competitors started swimming round and round in circles without going anywhere at all.

"What's happening, Rachel?" Kirsty asked, looking very perplexed.

"I suppose it might be something to do with the currents in the river," Rachel guessed. "But surely they wouldn't be *this* bad!"

The people watching had stopped
cheering and were now murmuring
to each other in surprise. Everyone,
including the girls, stared in amazement
as the swimmers bumped into each other,
their arms and legs getting all tangled up.

"Look at that boat, Kirsty," Rachel
said. "It's making things much worse!"

Kirsty saw that one of the stewards'
boats was floating around the swimmers,
getting in their way and making
everything even more chaotic.

"I thought the stewards were supposed to be *helping*!" Kirsty remarked as the boat chugged right past some of the swimmers, forcing them to move out of its way.

A sparkle on the surface of the river suddenly caught Rachel's eye, and she nudged Kirsty.

"There's *one* swimmer who seems OK," Rachel said. She pointed across the water. "See that boy, Kirsty? The one in the shiny swimming cap?"

Kirsty shaded her
eyes against the
sun and saw
one of the
competitors
powering
through
the water
towards
the yellow
marker. The
sunlight was
reflecting off
his dazzling silver
swimming cap.

"I wonder how *he's* managing to swim
in the right direction when everyone else
is getting in trouble," Kirsty said with
a frown.

"I think that boat's trying to catch up with him," said Rachel. The stewards' boat had now managed to get free of the crowd of hapless athletes, and it was sailing after the lone swimmer. At that moment, though, there was another announcement over the loudspeaker.

"Attention, everyone!" it boomed. "Due to unusual currents in the river, the race will be postponed while the organisers carry out some checks."

Rachel and Kirsty glanced at each other in disappointment.

"Oh, I feel so sorry for all the swimmers," sighed Kirsty.

"I expect the boy in the shiny swimming cap isn't too pleased," Rachel said. "He was really far out in front!"

As the girls watched, the stewards began to lower dinghies from their boats to pick up the floundering swimmers. It was then that Rachel noticed something very unusual. The clump of tall green reeds next to them was glowing with an amazing golden light.

"Kirsty!" Rachel whispered, nudging her friend. "See that? I think it really *is* magic!"

As Rachel spoke, a tiny glittering fairy peeped out from behind the reeds.

"Hello, girls," she called as Rachel and Kirsty caught their breath in excitement. "I'm Olympia the Games Fairy!"

Chapter Two
Games and Goblins

Olympia flew over to the girls, fluttering from reed to reed so that no one in the crowd would spot her. Finally she came to rest on the riverbank, and the girls sat down on the grass so that they could talk to her without being seen. Her golden hair sparkled in the sunlight and

she was wearing a smart lilac running outfit with a yellow tracksuit top.

"Oh, girls, I can't tell you how glad I am to see you!" Olympia exclaimed. "I've just come from the Fairyland Games, and everything's in *such* a mess!"

"The Fairyland Games?" Kirsty repeated. "What are they, Olympia?"

"We have swimming, cycling and running events," Olympia explained, "just like you're watching here today. It's my special responsibility to look after *all* games tournaments in both the human and the fairy worlds."

"You mean like this triathlon?" asked Rachel.

Olympia nodded. "I have three magical objects to help me," she explained. "The sparkling swimming cap makes all swimming events safe and fun. Then there's my musical bicycle bell – that ensures cycling races run smoothly. Finally, the tireless trainers make sure that all running events are enjoyable and successful."

"So what happened at the Fairyland Games?" Kirsty wanted to know.

"Well, the swimming event was just about to take place," Olympia said with a sigh, "but when the competitors dived into the water, they all began swimming around in circles or heading in the wrong direction! And that's when I discovered my sparkling swimming cap was missing."

Kirsty and Rachel exchanged excited glances. "That's exactly what's been happening here, too, Olympia," Rachel told her. "But everyone thinks the currents in the river are causing the swimmers' problems."

Olympia looked worried. "I *must* find

the sparkling swimming cap," she murmured anxiously. "If I don't, none of the swimming events at *any* of the human or fairy games will be a success!"

"Did Jack Frost and his goblins steal your sparkling swimming cap, Olympia?" asked Kirsty. Whenever there was a problem in Fairyland, it was usually because of cold-hearted Jack Frost and his naughty goblin servants. "Are they up to their old tricks again?"

"I'm not sure," Olympia replied slowly. "There *were* some goblins hanging around watching the Fairyland Games,

and I overheard them talking about
sneaking off to the human world to have
some fun. So I followed them here. I
don't know if they have the sparkling
swimming cap, but I *can* feel that it's
somewhere close by!"

"We'll help you look for it," Rachel
suggested. "I don't think the race will
start again for a while."

Kirsty, Rachel and Olympia glanced
across the water. The stewards' boats
were still floating around, picking up the
swimmers in their dinghies. Most of them
had been rescued by now, and Kirsty
could see that the only one left splashing
around in the water was the boy in the
shiny swimming cap. The boat that had
caused all the chaos earlier was now
almost level with him. The boy's silvery

swimming cap was glittering in a shaft of
sunlight, and as he raised his head from
the water to look up at the boat, Kirsty
caught a glimpse of a long green nose.
Shocked, she clapped her hand over
her mouth.

"Olympia,
I can see a
goblin in
the water,"
Kirsty said,
"and I
think he's
wearing your
sparkling
swimming
cap!"

Chapter Three
Dragonfly Disguise

Olympia took a long look at the lone swimmer in the water, and then her face broke into a huge smile.

"You're right, Kirsty," she declared. "Well spotted!"

"What now?" asked Rachel. "We *must* get the sparkling swimming cap from

that goblin!"

"I'll turn you into fairies," Olympia decided, "then we'll fly out to the goblin and try to snatch the cap before the boat picks him up. Does that sound like a good plan, girls?"

"That's a great idea," Kirsty replied.

But Rachel looked a bit worried. "There are a lot of people here to watch the triathlon," she pointed out. "What if someone sees us?"

"I've already thought of that," Olympia replied with a grin. "See all these dragonflies fluttering over the surface of the water? Well, we're going to be dragonflies, too!"

Olympia pointed her wand at Kirsty
and Rachel and a cloudy
mist of magical fairy dust
surrounded them. The
girls felt themselves
shrinking down
so quickly it
left them
breathless,
and in
just a few
seconds
they were
the exact same
size as Olympia. Kirsty
and Rachel also had their own pair of
translucent fairy wings on their backs.

But then, as they fluttered up into the

air with Olympia, the girls saw that with every movement, all their wings glittered with beautiful, shiny blue and green metallic sparkles.

"My fairy magic has given us a dragonfly disguise!" Olympia laughed. "Now let's go and stop that goblin getting away with my sparkling swimming cap!"

Olympia zoomed off across the river, and Rachel and Kirsty followed. They flew as

fast as they could, skimming the surface
of the water and dodging around the *real*
dragonflies on their way. But, to their
dismay, they weren't quite quick enough.
Ahead of them they could see that the
stewards' boat had already reached the
goblin swimmer.

"Oh my
goodness!"
Olympia
exclaimed
as they flew
closer. "Look,
girls - those
people on the
boat are goblins,
too. See their big
green ears poking out from under their
baseball caps?"

Rachel's heart sank as she realised that Olympia was right. Two of the goblins on the boat were struggling to untie the dinghy, while the third and biggest goblin was leaning over the side, shouting to the swimmer.

"It's *my* turn to wear the sparkling swimming cap now," the big goblin yelled, "so hand it over!"

The goblin swimmer was treading water, looking very sulky. "No way!" he muttered.

The big goblin glared at him. Suddenly he leaned further over the side and whipped the sparkling swimming cap right off the other goblin's head.

"Give that back!" howled the swimmer goblin as Olympia, Rachel and Kirsty hovered silently above them. The other two goblins on the boat saw what was happening. They immediately abandoned the dinghy and rushed over to the big goblin.

"*I* want to wear the sparkling swimming cap!" one of them roared, trying to grab it from him.

"No, me, me!" the other shrieked. Meanwhile the goblin in the water was climbing up the side of the boat. He jumped on to the deck and tried to snatch the sparkling swimming cap back from the big goblin. As all four goblins fought over it, the sparkling swimming cap slipped from their grasping fingers and over the side of the boat. It fell into the river with a splash, bobbing up and down in the water.

44

"Come on!" Olympia whispered to Rachel and Kirsty. "Now's our chance!"

"You idiots!" the big goblin shouted. "Quick, someone dive in and get it!"

Olympia, Rachel and Kirsty swooped down to the water, their eyes fixed on the sparkling swimming cap. They were determined to retrieve it before the goblins. But then Kirsty spotted a sleek dark-brown shape gliding silently through the water. It was an otter, and she was heading straight for the sparkling swimming cap. With one smooth movement, she grabbed it in her teeth, twisted around and swam off again.

Chapter Four
Inside the Otter's Den

"Oh no!" Olympia cried. "Girls, we must follow her!"

The three friends whizzed after the otter, skimming low across the surface of the water. Behind them they could hear the goblins moaning and groaning and blaming each other for the loss of the sparkling swimming cap.

"I wonder what the otter wants with a swimming cap, of all things?" Rachel said. The otter was swimming towards the opposite bank of the river, the sparkling swimming cap still clutched firmly in her mouth.

"I have no idea," Olympia admitted. "I just hope we can persuade her to give it back!"

The otter had now reached the riverbank. She scrambled out of the water and then slipped out of sight into a hole among a tangle of tree roots.

"She's gone into her holt," said Olympia, fluttering around outside the hole. "That's what an otter's home is called, girls. We'll have to follow her inside." She put a finger to her lips. "We must be very quiet, because we don't want to scare her."

Rachel and Kirsty nodded. Olympia flew into the hole and the girls went in straight after her.

It was very dark inside, but the magical glow from the tip of Olympia's wand helped to light their way a little. As they flew through several interconnecting passages, Kirsty was surprised by how warm and dry the holt felt.

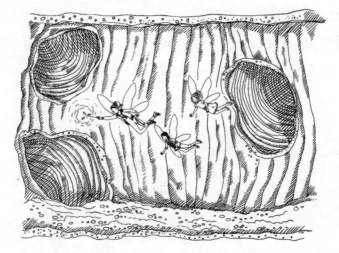

Suddenly the three friends saw a faint silvery light ahead of them. They had reached a big central chamber at the heart of the otter's den.

The otter was laying the sparkling swimming cap on the ground, smoothing it out with her paws. Olympia, Rachel and Kirsty smiled when they saw five adorable baby otters curled up in a ball together, watching their mother with big brown eyes.

"Come along, children," the otter said. "I've found you a lovely new cosy bed!" And she patted the sparkling swimming cap with her paw.

Rachel fluttered forward. "Excuse me," she said politely.

The otter looked around, and all the babies stared at Rachel.

"We're very sorry to bother you," Rachel went on, "but, you see, that swimming cap was stolen from our friend here, Olympia the Games Fairy. And she really *would* like it back."

"The sparkling swimming cap is *very* important," Kirsty chimed in. "Its magic helps all swimming events at games and tournaments to run smoothly. There'll be chaos without it!"

"I'm sorry," the otter replied, "but it's taken me *ages* to find my babies a comfy bed. I don't want to give it up!"

Chapter Five
Olympia's Lullaby

"Oh dear!" Olympia murmured.

"Olympia, listen," Rachel whispered in
her ear. "What about if you used your
magic to make an extra-special bed for
the otter's babies?"

"Great idea!" Kirsty agreed, and
Olympia nodded.

"We can see that you just want a gorgeous soft bed for your cute babies," Olympia told the otter. "So if you give us the cap back, I'll magic up the cosiest, softest and most comfortable bed in the whole world!"

Rachel, Kirsty and Olympia stared hopefully at the otter. What would she say, Kirsty wondered.

The otter thought about it for a few seconds.

"That's very kind of you," she said at last, her whiskers twitching a little. "You can have the swimming cap back."

Beaming, Olympia flew over to the sparkling swimming cap. The otters watched, wide-eyed, as she tapped the cap with her wand and the magical sparkles immediately returned it to its Fairyland size. Olympia picked up the swimming cap and tucked it safely under her arm.

"Thank you so much," Olympia said to the otter. "And now I shall keep my part of our bargain!"

Olympia waved her wand and sang:

Close your eyes, sleepyheads,
And lie down in your cosy bed,
Snuggle down, all warm and dry,
And listen to my lullaby.

As Rachel, Kirsty and the otters
watched, a mist of magical fairy dust
floated down from Olympia's wand and
landed on the ground.
Immediately,
a large
circular
nest of
moss and
grass, woven
with leaves and
feathers, appeared.

58

The little otters gave squeaks of delight and scampered over to clamber inside.

"That's a wonderful nest," the mother otter said gratefully. "Thank you."

"Goodbye!" called Olympia and the girls, waving as they flew out of the holt. "And sweet dreams!" Kirsty added.

Outside, Olympia, Rachel and Kirsty gazed across the river. They were all glad to see that the goblin boat had vanished.

"Girls, thank you *so* much for your help," Olympia said with a huge smile. "I must rush the sparkling swimming cap back to Fairyland so that the swimming event can go ahead."

"Can Kirsty and I stay as fairies for a little while?" Rachel asked. "We'll get a great view of all the triathlon events from high up in the air!"

"And we could keep an eye on those

goblins, too," Kirsty added.

"Of course," Olympia agreed. "I'll come back a bit later and change you back to your human size. Goodbye, girls!"

"See you soon," Rachel and Kirsty chorused as Olympia disappeared in a flurry of sparkles.

As the girls skimmed across the water, back to the other side of the river, they heard another announcement booming over the loudspeaker.

"Attention, everyone! The currents are now back to normal and the swimming race will restart in five minutes."

"Great!" Rachel said happily. "We've managed to save the first event of the day from being a total disaster!"

"Yes, but I wonder where those naughty goblins have gone," Kirsty replied. "I bet we haven't seen the last of them!"

Story Two
The Musical Bicycle Bell

Chapter Six
Bicycle Breakdown

"Wasn't that amazing?" Rachel said with a huge grin, as she and Kirsty applauded along with the rest of the excited crowd.

The swimming race had just finished and the girls had enjoyed the thrilling finale with three of the swimmers fighting it out for first place. Now those three swimmers were out of the water, drying themselves off as quickly as they could and pulling on their cycling shorts and helmets, ready for the bicycle race. Other competitors were also running out of the river as they completed their swims.

"If the bike race is as exciting as the swim, it'll be brilliant!" Kirsty declared. She and Rachel were still fairy-sized  and they were perched on a windowsill high up on one of the houses. The house was in the street that led down to the river and it was right at the start of the cyclists' route.

"We'll have a great view, and no one will notice us up here," Rachel said. "They'll be too busy watching the race!"

The girls leaned forward eagerly as the first athlete climbed onto his bike. Head down, he pedalled off with a determined look on his face. But he'd only gone a few metres when his bike began to wobble wildly from side to side.

"What's happening to my handlebars?" he cried, looking bewildered. He came to a halt and then held his handlebars up in the air. They'd become completely detached from his bicycle!

"Oh, what a shame," Kirsty said to Rachel. "Look, the other two are going to overtake him."

The swimmers who'd finished second and third were on their bikes now, too. They both sped off, only to stop abruptly with shouts of dismay. The front wheel had come off one of the bicycles and was rolling away down the street, while the chain had come loose from the other and was dragging on the ground.

"What's going on?" Rachel murmured, puzzled.

Most of the swimmers were now
pedalling off on their bicycles, but none
of them got more than a few metres
before something went wrong. Seats
began to fall off the bikes and crash
to the ground. Wheels, chains and
handlebars came loose and some of the
bicycles even started to go backwards,
although the cyclists were all
pedalling *forwards*.

The crowd looked on in amazement as one by one the competitors came to a halt and got off their bikes. It was a scene of total confusion.

"Attention, everyone!" The announcer whose voice was booming from the loudspeaker sounded just as astonished as everyone else. "In the interests of everyone's safety, the race has been stopped. It will begin again in ten minutes."

"I hope they give a head-start to the swimmers who came first," Kirsty remarked. "It won't be very fair otherwise."

"I wonder if this is something to do with those naughty goblins," Rachel said thoughtfully.

"I think you're right, Rachel!" Kirsty replied, her face lighting up with excitement. "Look!"

Kirsty pointed at the loudspeaker on the corner of the street. Rachel saw dazzling golden sparkles drifting out of it, and she smiled.

"Olympia's back!" Rachel announced as the fairy flew out of the mouth of the loudspeaker. She waved her wand in greeting at the girls and then zoomed towards them.

Kirsty was dismayed to see that their little friend looked very worried. "Has something happened in Fairyland, Olympia?" she asked.

"Because the bicycle race here is in complete chaos!" Rachel added.

Olympia sighed. "Girls, some of the goblins thought it would be great fun to steal my musical bicycle bell!" she explained. "That's why *all* cycling events have been disrupted – including the one that's about to take place in Fairyland. Will you help me to find the bell?"

"Of course we will!" Kirsty and Rachel said excitedly.

Chapter Seven
Super-Cyclists

Olympia looked relieved. "Thank you so much, girls," she replied. Then she glanced down the street. All the cyclists were gathered together in one large group, trying to fix their bikes with help from the officials.

"I think we should move away from

here," Olympia went on. "As there's no cycling race to watch at the moment, someone might glance up and spot us."

"The race route is that way," Kirsty said, pointing to a left turn in the street. "Shall we fly down one of these other roads? There won't be any crowds waiting there."

"Good idea," Olympia agreed.

Taking care to stay high up in the air, and keeping close to the houses, the three

friends flew quickly along the street. Then they turned the corner and flew down one of the side lanes. Kirsty was right. The lane was empty because it wasn't part of the race route.

"We can still see what's going on," Rachel said as they came to land on top of a lamppost. She pointed down the lane. The main street was at the end of it, and they could see some of the crowd waiting patiently for the race to restart.

"We'll fly back to join the crowds as soon as the race begins," Olympia promised. "I know the goblins must be around here somewhere. They'll

be super-cyclists now that they've got
the musical bicycle bell, so I'm sure that
they'll want to take part in the race!"

"When did the goblins steal the bell,
Olympia?" asked Kirsty.

"Just before the Fairyland bicycle

race was about to
start," Olympia
told her.

"Francesca the
Football Fairy saw
them running off
with it."

Rachel was still
gazing at the crowd
on the main street.
Suddenly she saw
five cyclists dressed in
brightly coloured shirts,

shorts and helmets slip out into the street from behind the crowd. They whizzed off on their bikes at great speed, heading for the lane where Rachel, Kirsty and Olympia were hiding.

"Why are those cyclists coming down here?" Rachel wondered aloud. "The race doesn't go this way. And, besides,

it hasn't even restarted yet!"

"Maybe they're having their own race," Kirsty suggested.

The cyclists were pedalling very fast and shooting along the lane at top speed. As they neared the lamppost where the fairies were sitting, one of the cyclists bashed into another one and knocked his helmet off. The friends gasped when they saw he had a green head!

"Goblins!" Kirsty breathed.

At that moment the goblin in the lead rang the silver bell on the front of his bicycle. The sound of a beautiful melody filled the air, and Rachel and Kirsty could see very faint sparkles of fairy magic drifting around the bell.

"That goblin has my musical bicycle bell fixed to his handlebars!" Olympia cried. "After him, girls!"

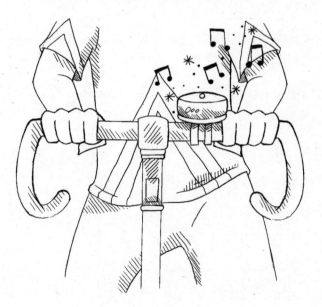

Chapter Eight
Grab that Bell!

Olympia, Rachel and Kirsty zoomed down from the lamppost. Then they chased after the goblins who were still pedalling so fast that their big green feet were just a blur.

"Do you think we can catch them and get the bell back?" Rachel whispered.

The goblins were so quick, it was quite difficult for Olympia and the girls to keep up with them.

"I'm not sure," Olympia murmured. "But we mustn't let them out of our sight, whatever we do!"

Kirsty realised that the goblins were racing around the empty streets that weren't part of the cycle route. That was lucky, she thought, as it meant there was no one around to notice them.

The goblin with Olympia's bell rang it again as he flew around the next corner.

"You've had the musical bicycle bell for ages," one of the other goblins complained, panting for air as he cycled along. "Let someone else have a go – like me!"

"*I* want the bell!" puffed the goblin whose helmet had fallen off. He'd stopped to collect it and now he was bringing up the rear. "It's *my* turn."

"Come and
get it then!"
the first
goblin
jeered.
He turned
to stick
his tongue
out at
the others
and then he
cycled off as
fast as he could.

The other goblins followed, all of them
still yelling and complaining.

"You know Jack Frost wants the silly
Games Fairy's bell so that he can win the
cycle race," shouted the second goblin,
"so you'd better not lose it."

"Yes, Jack Frost is *really* mad that the fairies got the sparkling swimming cap back again," the last goblin reminded them. "He was hoping one of us would win the race. He wants to win *everything*!"

"So Jack Frost told his goblins to steal my bell so that one of them can cheat and win the bicycle race!" Olympia murmured. "Girls, we must find a way to stop them!"

The goblins were still cycling around the empty streets. Although Olympia, Rachel and Kirsty were flying as fast as they could, they weren't able to catch up with the goblins who managed to stay a little way ahead of them. But then Rachel realised that they'd gone around in a big circle and were almost back where they'd started. The goblins were close to the official cycle route again, and they were heading towards the busy streets packed with people waiting to watch the race.

"We'll be back among the crowds in a minute or two," Rachel pointed out, looking worried. The goblins had now turned the corner and were heading along the lane where Olympia and the girls had first spotted them.

"They're going straight towards the main street," said Olympia. "We won't be able to follow them there – someone might spot us!"

"What are we going to do?" Kirsty said desperately. "If the goblins join the race when it's almost finished, they'll win by cheating!"

The goblins were now only a couple of metres away from the crowds on the main street. All of a sudden, the goblin at the back bent down from his bicycle and picked up a stick lying in the road. As Olympia and the girls watched, he put on a spurt and caught up with the goblin in front. He was cycling along smugly, loudly ringing the musical bicycle bell over and over again.

The goblin with the twig leaned over and stuck it in the spokes of the leading goblin's front wheel. The wheel stopped turning instantly, bringing the bicycle to a sudden halt. With a shriek of surprise, the goblin let go of the musical bicycle bell and went flying over the handlebars. He landed in the road with a groan, and his bicycle crashed down beside him.

"This is our chance to grab my bell, girls!" Olympia whispered.

But before Olympia, Rachel and Kirsty could do anything, a race official, who'd been standing on the corner of the lane, rushed towards the goblins. "What are you doing?" the official demanded with a frown. "The race hasn't re-started yet. You shouldn't be cycling around here, anyway. It's not part of the route."

He glared down at the groaning goblin who was now dusting himself off. "And was that you, ringing your bell so loudly all the time? That's against the rules, you know!"

Quickly the official bent down and removed the musical bicycle bell from the goblin's bicycle. "I'm confiscating this!" the official said. Then he slipped Olympia's bell into his pocket and hurried off.

Chapter Nine
Noise Annoys!

"Oh no!" Olympia gasped, horrified.
"What shall we do *now*, girls?"

"We'll just have to wait around and
hope we get a chance to take the bell
out of his pocket," Rachel sighed,
dismayed, as the official went back to his
post on the corner of the lane.

"But there are so many people around," Kirsty pointed out. "It's going to be *really* difficult."

Meanwhile the silly goblins were arguing furiously with each other. "This is all your fault!" one of them screeched at the goblin who'd had the bell. "*You* lost the musical bicycle bell, and *you're* the one who's going to have to tell Jack Frost!"

"I wouldn't have lost it if this idiot hadn't stuck a twig in my wheel," the goblin muttered, giving the one who'd done it a big shove.

"Yes, you would!" the other retorted, shoving him back. "That official said you're not allowed to ring your bicycle bell all the time so he would have taken it from you anyway. You were just showing off because you had the bell!"

"You're just a great big show-off!" the other goblins chorused.

As the goblins continued to yell at each other, Kirsty racked her brains, trying to think of a way to get the musical bicycle bell back without being seen.

"Oh!" she exclaimed suddenly. Rachel and Olympia glanced at her eagerly.

"Do you have an idea, Kirsty?" asked Olympia hopefully.

Kirsty nodded. "We can't fly over to the official and take the bell without being seen," she said slowly. "So maybe we could make him *throw* the bell away so that we can get it back?"

"How?" asked Rachel.

"By making the bell ring and ring without stopping!" Kirsty turned to Olympia.

"Could you do that with your magic, Olympia?"

Olympia smiled and nodded. She pointed her wand at the race official, and a stream of magical sparkles danced through the air towards his pocket.

Immediately the air was filled with the clear and beautiful sound of the musical bicycle bell. The official jumped with surprise and, fishing inside his pocket, he pulled the bell out.

Olympia and the girls watched as he tried to turn it off, but couldn't.

The musical bicycle bell was still ringing loudly. Everyone in the crowd was looking at the official, wondering why he didn't just turn it off, and even the goblins had stopped arguing and were watching curiously.

The official stared down helplessly at the musical bicycle bell as it tinkled away without a break. He shook it a few times, but when it still didn't stop, he looked around and spotted a litter bin behind him. Quickly he hurried over and threw the musical bicycle bell into the bin. Then, looking very embarrassed, he rushed back to his position.

"Hurry now, girls!" Olympia murmured.

The litter bin was hidden behind the race official who now had his back to them. Silently Olympia, Kirsty and Rachel zoomed down towards it.

"Look out!" Kirsty gasped as she saw the goblins rushing over to the bin, too.

The musical bicycle bell was lying on top of the litter in the bin and Olympia flew down to pick it up. But to Rachel and Kirsty's dismay, the goblins hurled themselves at the bin, desperate to seize the bell for themselves.

"Don't let them get it!" one of the goblins roared.

Chapter Ten
The Race Begins

All the goblins stuck their arms into the rubbish bin at exactly the same moment and ended up banging their heads together! As they yelled out in pain, Olympia swooped down between them and grabbed the musical bicycle bell. The instant Olympia touched the bell it

stopped ringing and shrank down to its
Fairyland size. Rachel and Kirsty sighed
with relief.

Olympia fluttered upwards with a
beaming smile,
clutching the bell.

One goblin
jumped up
in the air
to try and
catch her,
but he only
succeeded
in knocking
the bin over.
The rubbish
flew out and all the
goblins shrieked with rage as they were
covered in apple cores, sweet wrappers

and other bits of litter.

"Give us back the bell!" one goblin roared furiously.

Olympia shook her head as she, Rachel and Kirsty hovered above them. "Go home and tell Jack Frost that he

should learn how to be a good sport and *not* try to win races by cheating!" she told them.

The goblins moved away from the mess on the ground. They were grumbling and complaining so loudly that the

official glanced around to see what was going on. Instantly Olympia, Rachel and Kirsty zipped out of sight behind the bin.

"What are you doing *now*?" the official asked, hardly able to believe his eyes as he stared at the litter-covered goblins. "You should be lining up ready for the race to start."

"Go away!" one of the goblins muttered sulkily. "We don't want to be in the race now!"

Then, shaking themselves free of sweet wrappers, they all slouched grumpily away, leaving their bicycles behind.

"Girls, I can't thank you enough for all your help," Olympia declared, her eyes shining. "I was *so* worried we wouldn't be able to get my beautiful bell back – and then the cycling races here and in Fairyland would both have been ruined!"

"Ladies and gentlemen," the announcer said over the loudspeaker, "we are *very* pleased to tell you that the bikes have been fixed and we can now restart the race. Will the cyclists take up their positions, please?"

"Oh, great!" Rachel exclaimed. "It looks like everything is back to normal."

"Girls, would you like to come back to Fairyland with

me to return the musical bicycle bell?"
asked Olympia. "Then you can stay and
watch our races, too."

"We'd love to!" Kirsty agreed eagerly,
and Rachel nodded.

With a smile Olympia waved her
wand. In the twinkling of an eye all
three of them were swept up in a cloud
of glittering magic and whisked away
to Fairyland.

Story Three
The Tireless Trainers

Chapter Eleven
Ready, Steady, But NOT Go!

Just a few seconds later Olympia, Rachel and Kirsty arrived in the open-air sports stadium in Fairyland. King Oberon and Queen Titania were seated in the Royal Box, and the stadium was packed with fairies who were there to watch the races.

"Rachel and Kirsty have helped me to

find the musical bicycle bell!" Olympia announced, holding up the bell. The fairies all cheered and applauded.

The girls watched as Olympia flew over to the Royal Box. At the front of the box were three plinths, one bronze, one silver and one gold.

Carefully Olympia placed the musical bicycle bell on the bronze plinth. Rachel and Kirsty could see the sparkling swimming cap on the silver stand, and on the shining gold plinth was a pair of dazzling golden trainers. They glittered with fairy magic in the sunshine.

"Those must be the tireless trainers," Rachel said, as she and Kirsty admired them. "They look amazing!"

"They're the sparkliest trainers I've ever seen!" Kirsty replied.

King Oberon and Queen Titania stood up and waved to Rachel and Kirsty.

"Thank you, girls, and thank you,

Olympia," King Oberon called. "We've had to delay our races because of those naughty goblins, but now we can continue with our games."

"You're very welcome here, Rachel and Kirsty," Queen Titania added with a sweet smile. "We were just about to start the running race. And after that we'll hold the swimming and cycling races. Please do find seats and join us!"

The fairies in the stadium clapped once more as Olympia, Rachel and Kirsty sat down in the front row.

Looking around, Rachel could see lots
of their old friends in the audience. She
waved hello to India the Moonstone
Fairy, Crystal the Snow Fairy and
Willow the Wednesday Fairy, who were
sitting nearby.

Then Bertram the frog footman
stepped forward onto the running track.

"It is time for the
running race to take
place," Bertram
announced, and
there was another
burst of cheering.
"Our contestants
today are the
Rainbow Fairies!"
the frog footman
went on.

Delighted, Rachel turned to Kirsty as Ruby, Amber, Saffron, Fern, Sky, Izzy and Heather jogged onto the running track. "There are lots of our fairy friends here," Rachel pointed out, "but the Rainbow Fairies are our oldest friends of all!"

Kirsty smiled. "We had our very first magical adventure with them, didn't we, Rachel?" she remembered. "I wonder

who's going to win?"

The seven Rainbow Fairies went over to the starting line. There was an air

of great excitement in the stadium as all
the fairies, including Rachel and Kirsty,
leaned forward eagerly in their seats to
watch the race.

Bertram cleared his throat. "On your
marks!" he called.

The seven fairies took up their positions
on the track.

"Ready!" Bertram went on. "Steady!"
He paused. "GO!"

The Rainbow Fairies surged forward
and everyone in the stadium began
to shout encouragement. But almost
immediately Ruby and Amber stumbled
and fell at exactly the same moment.

"Our laces have been tied together!"
Amber yelled, as she and Ruby rolled
around on the track,
unable to pull free
of each other.
Meanwhile
Fern and
Sky had
stopped,
too. They
were both
hopping
around,
trying to

pull their trainers off.
Rachel and Kirsty
watched them
anxiously. What
was going
on, Kirsty
wondered.
"My
trainers are
too small!"
Fern
groaned.
"Mine, too,"
Sky agreed. "Ow! They're pinching my
toes!"

Saffron, Izzy and Heather had run
off along the track, leaving the others
behind. But then Saffron gave a yelp
of distress.

"Oh no! My trainers have got too BIG!" she cried.

Rachel and Kirsty looked down at Saffron's trainers. They were now as big as clowns shoes! Saffron couldn't run in them and ended up tripping and falling.

"Help!" Izzy shrieked, coming to a halt herself and staring down at her bare feet. "My trainers have disappeared!"

"And *one* of my trainers has vanished, too," added Heather, hopping around in her remaining shoe.

Olympia frowned. "Everything's going wrong!" she murmured to Rachel and Kirsty.

Chapter Twelve
Keep on Running!

As Bertram and the other frog footmen
rushed to help the Rainbow Fairies,
Rachel saw another old friend hurrying
towards them. It was Samantha the
Swimming Fairy.

"Hello, girls!" she gasped, looking
very distressed. "Thank you so much

for helping Olympia to find the sparkling swimming cap. I'm so glad the swimming race can go ahead. But now we have another problem!"

Samantha turned and pointed to the golden plinth that stood underneath the Royal Box.

"The tireless trainers have gone!" Kirsty exclaimed, her eyes wide with surprise and alarm. "But they were there a minute ago."

"So that's why the running race is

going wrong!"
Olympia
murmured,
biting
her lip.
"Was it
the goblins
again?"

Samantha
shook her head. "No, it was Jack Frost
himself!" she explained. "He sneaked
into the stadium while everyone was
busy cheering and stole the trainers a few
moments before the race began. I don't
think anybody spotted him except me."

King Oberon and Queen Titania had
now been told that the tireless trainers
were no longer on the golden stand
under the Royal Box. Some of the fairies

in the audience had also realised that
the trainers were gone, and they were
murmuring anxiously to each other.

"This is awful!" Olympia sighed,
looking completely devastated. "Jack
Frost is so cunning and sly! What on
earth shall we do *now*?"

"Don't worry, Olympia," Kirsty
comforted her. "Rachel and I will help
you to get the tireless trainers back."

"Of course we will," Rachel agreed.
"I bet Jack Frost has taken
them to his Ice
Castle!"

Olympia
brightened up
a little. "Your
Majesties,"
she called, as

she and the girls fluttered over to the Royal Box. "Jack Frost sneaked into the stadium and stole the tireless trainers, but Rachel, Kirsty and I are determined to get them back!"

Cheers and whoops rang out around the stadium at Olympia's words.

"Take care, all of you," Queen Titania cried, waving as Olympia, Rachel and Kirsty left the stadium.

"And be on your guard for more of

FAIRY GAMES

Jack Frost's tricks!" said King Oberon.

Olympia and the girls flew over the lush green meadows and hills and the sparkling rivers of Fairyland. Very soon, though, they left the beautiful countryside behind. Now they were in a cold land of freezing grey mists, icy frosts and snow. Jack Frost's castle, built of huge glistening blocks of ice, loomed up ahead of them through the gloom. The girls had been to the Ice Castle many times before, but seeing it still sent a nervous shiver down Rachel's spine.

"How are we going to get inside?"

Kirsty asked as she, Olympia and Rachel
hovered near the entrance.

"I'm not sure," Olympia began. Then
she gasped as the doors began to open.
"Hide, girls, quickly!"

The three friends zoomed upwards
and ducked down behind one of the icy
turrets. Then they peeped around the
wall to see who was coming out. To
her surprise, Kirsty saw Jack Frost come

running out
of the castle.
He was
wearing a
singlet and
shorts, and on
his feet were
the dazzling
tireless

trainers. Kirsty nudged Rachel and Olympia, and pointed silently at Jack Frost's feet.

Jack Frost was followed out by a crowd of his goblin servants. As he ran up and down outside the castle entrance, the goblins milled around him. They all looked rather worried.

"Do something!" Jack Frost roared furiously as he ran round and round in circles. "Anything!"

"What's going on?" Rachel whispered, puzzled. The goblins were now dashing about in a panic, bumping into Jack Frost and each other.

"The powerful magic of my tireless trainers means that Jack Frost can't stop running!" Olympia exclaimed.

Chapter Thirteen
The Terrible Trainers!

Jack Frost was now running frantically in a circle. His normally pale blue face was red and he was panting hard.

"Get these terrible trainers off my feet!" he bellowed at the panicking goblins. "NOW!"

"I've got an idea!" a big goblin yelled.

Gathering a couple of the others around him, he whispered his plan to them, and then they all charged into the Ice Castle. A few moments later Olympia, Rachel and Kirsty saw them come out carrying a large net.

"We're going to try and catch you," the goblin explained to Jack Frost.

"Well, get on with it then!" Jack Frost shouted rudely.

The goblins ran up to Jack Frost and

tried to hurl the net over him. But at the last moment the tireless trainers sent him scooting away in the opposite direction. Instead of capturing Jack Frost, the net fell over some other goblins.

"Help!" shrieked a goblin caught in the net. "Get us out of here!"

The big goblin freed the ones who were

trapped by the net, and then he and his
friends made another attempt to snare
Jack Frost. This time, though, they
managed to tangle *themselves* up in the
net. Olympia and the girls giggled.

"You fools!"
Jack Frost
snarled as
he raced
around his
Ice Castle.
"You're
all in big
trouble
now!"

"Let me
help!" shouted
a goblin with
big ears. As

Jack Frost ran past him, he leapt forward and tried to rugby tackle him to the ground. Unfortunately another goblin had had the same idea, and he dived for Jack Frost at the very same moment. The goblins ended up in a heap of tangled arms and legs as Jack Frost sprinted away.

"STOP!" Jack Frost shrieked, glaring down at the tireless trainers. "I order you to

STOP!" But still he continued to circle
the Ice Castle at top speed.

"However are we going to get the
trainers back?" Rachel asked with a

frown. "There doesn't seem to be any
way Jack Frost is going to slow down!"

As Jack Frost ran towards the castle
entrance again, he glanced up and

spotted Olympia, Rachel and Kirsty
hovering above him. He gave a shout
of rage.

"You fairies!" Jack Frost panted
furiously. "Come down here immediately
and help me!"

"We will," Olympia agreed, "*if* you
return the tireless trainers."

Jack Frost scowled. "No, no, NO!"
he yelled. "I want to win *everything*,

and you pesky fairies aren't going
to stop me!" Then he pointed his ice
wand at the trainers, zapping them with
his magic.

"Stop it!" Olympia
called. "You can't
stop the tireless
trainers with just
any old magic
spell!"

But Jack
Frost took
no notice
and
continued
to try out
all his spells.

Suddenly he shrieked with surprise as an
ice bolt whisked him off his feet and flew

him out of sight.

"Jack Frost's random magic has taken him back to the human world!" Olympia sighed, lifting her own wand. "Come on, girls, we must follow him!"

Chapter Fourteen
A Very Strange Prize

With one wave of Olympia's wand, a single burst of fairy magic carried the three friends back to Melford.

"Look, the cycling race is over and the running race has already started," Rachel said as she, Olympia and Kirsty looked down on the main street.

There was a crowd of runners heading towards the finishing line, where a small podium had been set up, ready for the medals ceremony. There were three judges sitting there, waiting to present the prizes.

"And there's Jack Frost!" Olympia exclaimed, pointing with her wand. "He's appeared right in the middle of the pack of runners!"

Rachel and Kirsty could see Jack Frost running along with the other athletes.

But then, to their
dismay, the
runners
began
having
problems
with their
trainers,
stumbling
or tripping or
falling over, just as the Rainbow Fairies
had done. The watching crowd began to
murmur to each other in surprise as Jack
Frost shot out in front.

"The race is nearly over, and Jack
Frost's going to win!" Kirsty cried. Jack
Frost was sprinting towards the
finishing line as the other runners
struggled after him.

"Maybe the organisers will stop the race, like they did with the swimming and cycling," Rachel said.

Olympia shook her head. "I don't think they will because it's almost finished," she replied.

"What are we going to do?" asked Kirsty. "We don't have a chance of

grabbing the tireless trainers with all these people watching."

"Let's wait for Jack Frost to collect his winner's medal," Olympia suggested. "He'll go back to his Ice Castle afterwards, and then we can follow him."

Jack Frost was grinning widely and waving at the crowds as he passed by. Arms in the air, he crossed the finishing line and crowed with triumph. "I won!" Jack Frost boasted. "Clever old me!" "Only because you're wearing my tireless trainers," Olympia murmured with a sigh.

"Hello, you there!" One of the race organisers strode over to Jack Frost. "You're disqualified!"

Jack Frost looked furious. "Why?" he demanded, jogging up and down as the other runners began to limp and stumble across the finishing line.

"Because you appeared in the middle of all the other runners right at the end!" the organiser snapped. "*And* you're not even wearing an official number." He glared at Jack Frost. "You're disqualified!" he repeated and walked off.

"Look at Jack Frost," Rachel whispered to Kirsty and Olympia. "He's really annoyed!"

Jack Frost looked very sulky indeed. He rushed over to the podium with the other competitors and ran furiously up and down on the spot as one of the judges stepped forward with the microphone.

"Well, what a very eventful triathlon this has been!" the judge said with a smile. The crowd smiled and applauded. "I'm delighted to say that despite all the problems we've experienced today, this has been one of our best triathlons ever. We're going to present our winners with their medals now . . ."

Kirsty saw Jack Frost scowl icily.

"But first we have a *very* special prize to present," the judge went on. "The prize is for 'Bad Sport of the Day!'"

The crowd cheered.

"And our winner is the runner who only appeared at the end of the race!" the judge went on. He pointed at Jack Frost. "Would you come and collect your prize, please?"

Jack Frost's face lit up. "I *am* a winner after all!" he yelled happily. He dashed forwards and shook hands with the judge while running on the spot. Then the judge solemnly handed Jack Frost a  large, wilting green cabbage.

The crowd burst out laughing and so did Olympia, Kirsty and Rachel.

However, Jack
Frost was delighted.
Clutching his
cabbage, he ran
down the steps of the
podium again and
off down the street.
"After him,
girls!" Olympia
whispered.
Jack Frost
had turned off
the main street now and was jogging
along one of the empty lanes. Olympia
and the girls flew to catch up with him,
and when they did, Rachel could see
that he was very tired. He was puffing
and panting and even his spiky hair was
beginning to droop with exhaustion.

"Please help me!" Jack Frost gasped when he saw them. "I'll give you these terrible trainers if only you can get them off my feet so I can rest!"

"Very well," Olympia agreed. "Now the only problem we have is how to get the trainers off!"

Chapter Fifteen
The Medals Ceremony

Olympia turned to Rachel and Kirsty. "Any ideas, girls?" she asked hopefully, as Jack Frost ran wearily around them.

Kirsty stared down at the tireless trainers. It would be impossible to remove them while Jack Frost was running around, she thought. But what if his feet *weren't* on the ground at all?

"I think I have an idea!" Kirsty cried. She fluttered over to Jack Frost. "Can you do a handstand up against that wall over there?"

Jack Frost glared at her. "This is no time for games!" he snapped.

"It's not a game!" Kirsty replied. "If you do a handstand, we'll be able to untie the trainers and take them off your feet."

"Brilliant idea, Kirsty!" Olympia
declared.

Jack Frost ran over
to the wall, put
his hands down
on the ground
and then flipped
himself up into
a handstand. He
was still running,
but in midair,
and holding himself
up with
his scrawny arms.

Rachel and Kirsty dodged
around Jack Frost's waving feet and
undid the laces on both of the tireless
trainers. Jack Frost wobbled a little but

managed not to fall over. Then Olympia
swooped in and with Rachel and Kirsty's
help, she pulled off
the left trainer.
It immediately
shrank down to
its Fairyland size.
Next Olympia
and the girls
pulled off the right
trainer, and that
also shrank, becoming
the same size as the other.
Jack Frost gasped loudly
with relief as he flipped himself upright
again. "Thank goodness!" he groaned.
"I'm going home to have a long rest!"
Then he waved his wand and an ice bolt
carried him swiftly off to his castle.

"Girls, you were amazing!" Olympia announced. "I couldn't have got the trainers *or* my other magical objects back without your help. Will you come back to Fairyland with me  again to watch our races?"

"We'd love to, but we'd better not," Rachel sighed. "Now that the triathlon's over, my parents will be looking for us."

"Go and enjoy the rest of the medals

ceremony, then," Olympia told the girls with a smile. "And I'm sure all your friends in Fairyland will see you again very soon!"

Then, holding the tireless trainers, she vanished in a sparkling mist of magical fairy dust.

"Wasn't that just the most exciting competition *ever?*" Rachel said, as she and Kirsty ran hand in hand to watch the medals ceremony.

"I hope we go to lots more triathlons,"

Kirsty replied, "but I don't think we'll ever go to *quite* such an amazing one as this, thanks to Olympia and our fairy friends!"

The End

**Now it's time for Kirsty and
Rachel to help ...**

Paula the Pumpkin Fairy

Read on for a sneak peek ...

"This is the perfect place to spend
Halloween," said Rachel Walker,
looking around at the pumpkin field.

Rachel was staying with her best
friend, Kirsty Tate, for the weekend.
Kirsty's mum had just dropped them
off for the Big Pumpkin Patch Pick at
Pumpkin Patch Farm on the outskirts of
Wetherbury.

"We always manage to do something
fun on Halloween," said Kirsty.

The girls shared a smile, remembering
how they had met Trixie the Halloween
Fairy and helped her to stop Jack Frost

from spoiling the day for everyone. They had shared many magical adventures together, because the fairies often asked for their help when Jack Frost got up to mischief.

"I can't wait to pick our pumpkins," said Rachel. "I want to make the spookiest lantern ever."

The farmer was a friendly man in wellies and a thick jumper. He grinned at the families who had gathered in the field.

"Good morning, and welcome to our first Big Pumpkin Patch Pick," he said. "My name is Peter Pine. There are lots of fun things to do here today, starting with finding your perfect pumpkin to carve. They have been picked and lined up in rows. All you have to do is choose one!"

Kirsty knew many of the other children there, but she didn't recognise a tall, blonde girl who was standing apart from the other children. She had folded her arms and was scowling at the farmer.

"I wonder why she looks so cross," Rachel said.

"My mum says that sometimes people who seem angry are actually really unhappy underneath," said Kirsty. "If we can get past her grumpiness, there's probably someone really lovely inside."

Rachel smiled.

"Let's try to make friends with her," she whispered.

"These beauties were planted at the beginning of June," Mr Pine continued. "Pumpkins take three or four months to grow, and that's why they're so ripe and orange now."

Kirsty stepped closer to the blonde girl and smiled at her.

"Hi," she said.

"Leave me alone," the girl mumbled.

"We only want to say hello," Kirsty went on. "This is Rachel and I'm Kirsty. What's your name?"

"Polly," she said with a glare. "Now you've said hello, you can leave me alone."

As she turned away, Rachel saw tears glinting in her eyes.

"You're right," she said to Kirsty in a low voice. "I think she needs a friend."

She touched Polly's arm and tried again.

"Would you like to choose your pumpkin with us?" she asked.

"I hate pumpkins," Polly retorted.

"Oh," said Kirsty. "So, er, why have you come?"

"I had to," said Polly. "I live here. My dad bought this silly place and made me leave the city and come and live here."

"Wetherbury is lovely," said Kirsty. "I'm sure you'll like it if you give it a chance."

"Who owns that dog?" called out Mr Pine.

A little brown-and-white dog was scampering across the far end of the pumpkin patch. No one replied, but Rachel saw Polly staring at the animal until it disappeared into another field.

"Polly, could you help me?" called Mr Pine. "Some of the pumpkins seem to have gone missing."

Polly stomped off, muttering under her breath. Rachel and Kirsty started walking along the row, looking at one round, ripe pumpkin after another.

Read Paula the Pumpkin Fairy to find out what adventures are in store for Kirsty and Rachel!

Calling all parents, carers and teachers!
The Rainbow Magic fairies are here to help
your child enter the magical world of reading.
Whatever reading stage they are at, there's
a Rainbow Magic book for everyone!
Here is Lydia the Reading Fairy's guide to
supporting your child's journey at all levels.